AUTHOR DEDICATION

For Stephen Elizabeth Ira

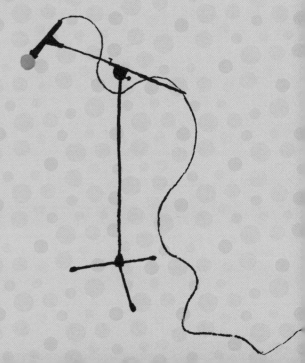

Reycraft Books
55 Fifth Avenue
New York, NY 10003
Reycraftbooks.com

Reycraft Books is a trade imprint and trademark of Newmark Learning, LLC.

Text copyright © 2019 by Kyle Lukoff

Illustration copyright © 2019 by Reycraft Books, an imprint of Newmark Learning, LLC

Library of Congress Cataloging-in-Publication Data is available.

ISBN: 978-1-4788-6789-0

Printed in Guangzhou, China
4401/0919/CA21901753

10 9 8 7 6 5 4 3 2 1

First Edition Hardcover published by Reycraft Books

Max

and the Talent Show

BY KYLE LUKOFF • ILLUSTRATED BY LUCIANO LOZANO

Chapter 1

My name is Max. I love to read.

My favorite books are comic books.

I also like funny books.

Sometimes I read stories about magic or adventure.

I don't like sad books.

I have a friend named Steven.
He likes to make up his own stories.
He always has a lot of ideas.

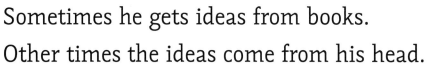

Sometimes he gets ideas from books.
Other times the ideas come from his head.

Steven makes me play dress up with him.

He gives me clothes that match his stories.

Once I was a pirate.

Another time I was a shark.

Sometimes he wants me to put on a dress.
I used to wear dresses but now I don't.
So I always say no.

When I play with other friends we run races.

And jump rope. And climb trees.

But when I play with Steven he wants to make up stories.

So he tells stories as we play.

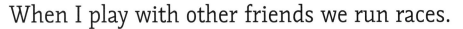

He will say that a train is chasing us.

We run away as fast as we can.

Or he will say that we are crossing a volcano.

We hop and jump across the lake of fire.

If we climb a tree, Steven will say we are in outer space.

We talk to aliens on the moon.

Steven and I go on a lot of adventures.

Chapter 2

There is another big difference between me and Steven.

He loves to be in the center of things.
I don't like being watched.

The school talent show is coming up.
I don't want to be in it.

But I don't want to be left out.

Steven puts his name on the sign-up sheet.

"I'll be a star!" he says.

"Do you want to be a star, too?"

I think about what I would do.

I don't like to sing. I don't dance. I don't play piano.

But I do like to help my friends.

"I'll be your assistant," I tell Steven.

"What does an assistant do?"

"It means I help you put on a show."

Steven likes that idea.
He loves to put on a show.
And he loves to tell me what to do.

"First I need to find a dress," says Steven.
His mom drives us to the mall.

The people who work at the store think the dress is for me.
They don't want to let Steven try it on.
But then he tells them a story. He tells them about a girl
in a beautiful dress. She was stolen by goblins.
If he can find a dress like hers, it will help him find her.

They love the story.
Steven gets to pick his favorite dress.
I think it looks like an upside-down ice cream cone.
But I don't tell Steven this.

"Are you going to sing for the talent show?" I ask,
but Steven is admiring his gown.

Then we go to the shoe store.

The shoe salesman doesn't like my stompy boots.

And he tells Steven not to try on high heels.

But Steven tells him a story about his grandmother.

He says she was the most famous actress in the world.

He says that her last wish was to find the shoes

she wore in her first movie.

Taken away by his words, the salesman gives Steven
a pair of shoes. They have heels that click on the floor.
"Are you going to dance in the talent show?" I ask.
Steven doesn't answer.
He is listening to the shoes as they click.

15

Steven tells a story
to find the perfect cape.
And a story for the perfect tiara.
"Are you going to play
the piano?" I ask.
I don't even know
if he plays the piano.

But Steven doesn't hear me.

He tilts the tiara so it sits just so. It glitters in the light.

I wonder what he is going to do for the talent show.

Chapter 3

It is the night of the talent show.

I help Steven zip up his ice-cream dress.

He slips his feet into the clicking heels.

I tie the cape around his neck.

He places the tiara on his head just so.

"What is your act?" I ask. Steven doesn't answer.
He is smiling at himself in the mirror.

The teacher in charge calls kids by name.
One recites a poem.
I don't understand it.

Another does splits and cartwheels.
It looks very hard.

Someone plays the violin.
It sounds like two cats fighting.

I don't know what my job is now.

Steven doesn't say he needs help.

When his name is called he clicks onto the stage.

"What are you doing tonight, young man?" the teacher asks.
Steven stares at the audience. He looks nervous.
And surprised.

And that's when I know.
He didn't choose a song. He didn't learn a dance.
He didn't bring an instrument.

He doesn't have a plan.

But he picked me to be his assistant.
What is my friend good at?
I think. And then I know.

"*Steven!*" I whisper loudly. "*Tell them the story!*"

Will he know what I mean?

He hears me. Steven stands up straight.

He doesn't look scared anymore.

In a strong voice he says, "I will tell you a story.

I will tell you a story of a stolen child. I will tell you about a movie star.

I will tell you about a lost treasure and a found kingdom."

And he does. His voice fills the room.

At the end, they live happily ever after.

My ears fill with the thunder of hands clapping.

Steven bows. He walks off the stage.

His tiara glitters in the light.

His cape flows behind him. His heels click on the floor.

He hugs me tight.

Then he pulls me out onto the stage. Everyone is still clapping.

He bows again. He makes me bow with him.

Everyone is looking at me too. It feels okay.

But I'm glad when we walk off the stage again.

"I couldn't have done that without you," he says.

"I know," I tell him. "That's why I'm your assistant."

Kyle Lukoff has worked at the intersection of books and people for over half his life, first as a bookseller, then as a school librarian, and now as a writer. He is transgender, like Max, and lives in a small Brooklyn apartment with six overflowing bookshelves.

Luciano Lozano was born the same year Man traveled to the Moon. That may be the reason why he has traveled a lot since childhood. When not traveling, he lives in Barcelona. His illustrations reflect his strong sense of color and texture, as well as his subtle sense of humor.